For my mother, Anne, whose song I still hear in the wind —G.M.

Viking
Published by Penguin Group
Penguin Young Readers Group, 345 Hudson Street, New York, New York 10014, U.S.A.
Penguin Group (Canada), 90 Eglinton Avenue East, Suite 700, Toronto, Ontario, Canada M4P 2Y3
(a division of Pearson Penguin Canada Inc.)
Penguin Books Ltd, 80 Strand, London WC2R 0RL, England
Penguin Ireland, 25 St Stephen's Green, Dublin 2, Ireland (a division of Penguin Books Ltd)
Penguin Group (Australia), 250 Camberwell Road, Camberwell, Victoria 3124, Australia
(a division of Pearson Australia Group Pty Ltd)
Penguin Books India Pvt Ltd, 11 Community Centre, Panchsheel Park, New Delhi – 110 017, India
Penguin Group (NZ), 67 Apollo Drive, Rosedale, Auckland 0632, New Zealand
(a division of Pearson New Zealand Ltd.)
Penguin Books (South Africa) (Pty) Ltd, 24 Sturdee Avenue, Rosebank, Johannesburg 2196, South Africa

Penguin Books Ltd, Registered Offices: 80 Strand, London WC2R 0RL, England

First published in 2012 by Viking, a division of Penguin Young Readers Group

1 3 5 7 9 10 8 6 4 2

LIBRARY OF CONGRESS CATALOGING-IN-PUBLICATION DATA
Marino, Gianna.
Meet me at the moon / by Gianna Marino.
p. cm.
Summary: During a dry time, Mama leaves Little One alone while she climbs the highest mountain to ask the skies for rain,
but she promises that her love will remain all around.
ISBN 978-0-670-01313-5 (hardcover)
[1. Mother and child—Fiction. 2. Separation (Psychology)—Fiction. 3. Elephants—Fiction. 4. Drought—Fiction. 5. Africa—Fiction.] I. Title.
PZ7.M33882Mee 2012   [E]—dc22   2011013210

Manufactured in China   Set in Old Claude   Book design by Nancy Brennan

Meet Me at the MOON

by Gianna Marino

VIKING
An Imprint of Penguin Group (USA) Inc.

Beneath the shade of the baobab tree, Little One sang the calling song, and Mama came with a loving nuzzle. "The land is dry, Little One," Mama said. "I must climb the highest mountain to ask the skies for rain."

"But Mama!" said Little One, "I don't want you to go."

"I know, Little One. But you will feel my love in everything around you."

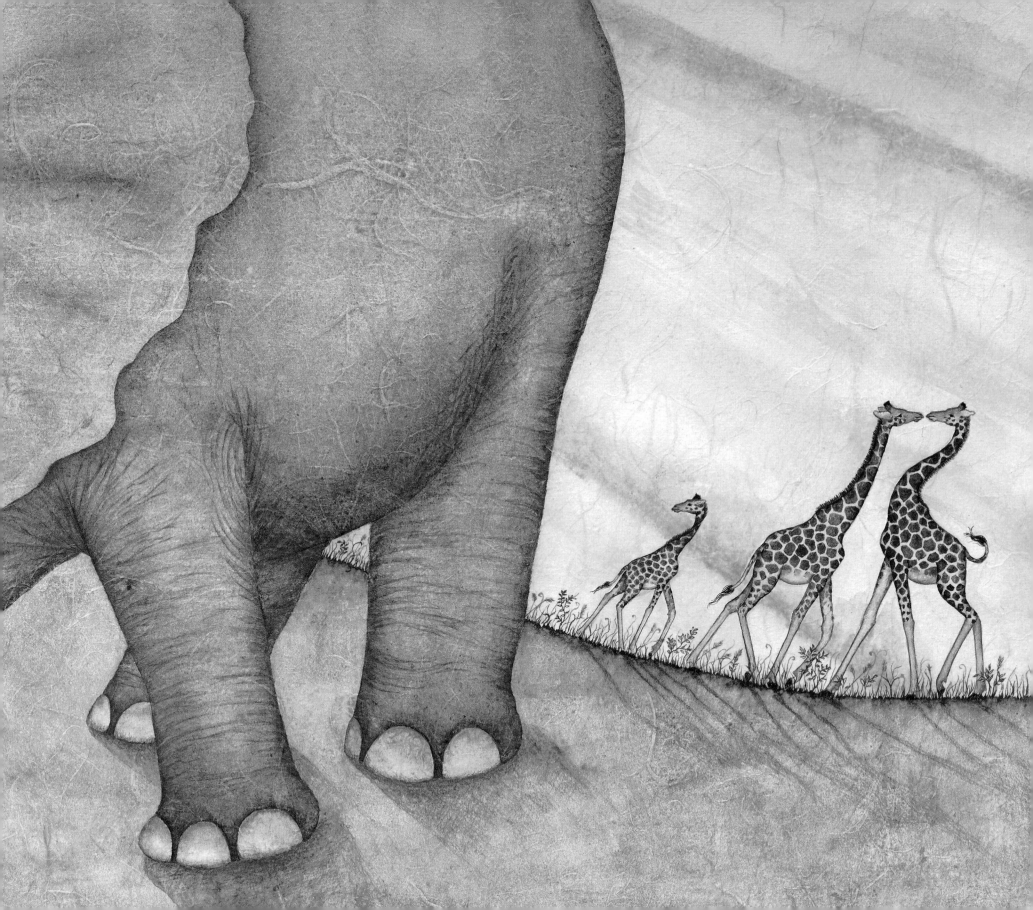

"What if I can't hear you, Mama?"

"Listen for my sound on the wind, Little One.
I will sing to you."

"How will I know that you still love me?"
asked Little One.

"I love you like the sun loves the earth," said
Mama. "When you feel the warmth of the sun,
I will be loving you from where I am."

"But Mama, I won't be able to see you."

"Find the brightest star, Little One. If we both look at the same star, it will be as if we are seeing each other."

"Mama?" said Little One. "How will you find me again?"

"When the night sky is bright, Little One, meet me
at the moon, where the sky touches the earth."

"I love you, Little One," said Mama.
Then Mama left to climb the highest mountain
to ask the skies for rain.

Each night, Little One found the brightest star,
knowing Mama was looking at the same star in her sky.
Each day, Little One listened to the wind and heard
Mama's song.

And as the sun warmed the earth, Little One felt loved.

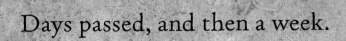

Days passed, and then a week.

The dry earth crumbled in the heat, and still
Mama did not return.

Dark clouds finally rolled across the sky and cracked open with rain.

But now there was no song on the wind.

No bright star to see.

No sun to make Little One feel warm and loved.

After a long while, the clouds parted.
Little One saw the moon, high in the sky.

"Mama, you told me you'd meet me at the moon," Little One said. "But how can I reach it?"

Then Little One remembered to sing the calling song, and sang deep into the night.

Slowly, the moon dropped and lit a path across the plains.
Little One saw something move in the light.

"Mama?" cried Little One.

When the moon touched the earth, Mama
answered with the calling song.

"You are in my most secret heart, Little
One," she sang.

"And you are in mine," Little One answered.

"I love you."